Put Beginning Readers on the Right Track with
ALL ABOARD READING™

The All Aboard Reading series is especially designed for beginning readers. Written by noted authors and illustrated in full color, these are books that children really want to read—books to excite their imagination, expand their interests, make them laugh, and support their feelings. With fiction and nonfiction stories that are high interest and curriculum-related, All Aboard Reading books offer something for every young reader. And with four different reading levels, the All Aboard Reading series lets you choose which books are most appropriate for your children and their growing abilities.

Picture Readers

Picture Readers have super-simple texts, with many nouns appearing as rebus pictures. At the end of each book are 24 flash cards—on one side is a rebus picture; on the other side is the written-out word.

Station Stop 1

Station Stop 1 books are best for children who have just begun to read. Simple words and big type make these early reading experiences more comfortable. Picture clues help children to figure out the words on the page. Lots of repetition throughout the text helps children to predict the next word or phrase—an essential step in developing word recognition.

Station Stop 2

Station Stop 2 books are written specifically for children who are reading with help. Short sentences make it easier for early readers to understand what they are reading. Simple plots and simple dialogue help children with reading comprehension.

Station Stop 3

Station Stop 3 books are perfect for children who are reading alone. With longer text and harder words, these books appeal to children who have mastered basic reading skills. More complex stories captivate children who are ready for more challenging books.

In addition to All Aboard Reading books, look for All Aboard Math Readers™ (fiction stories that teach math concepts children are learning in school) and All Aboard Science Readers™ (nonfiction books that explore the most fascinating science topics in age-appropriate language).

All Aboard for happy reading!

To my daughter "Kristinella" with love,
your Queen Mother!

Library of Congress Cataloging-in-Publication Data

Cocca-Leffler, Maryann, 1958-
   Princess for a day / by Maryann Cocca-Leffler.
     p.   cm.—(All aboard reading. Level 1)
   Summary: Jessie becomes a princess complete with a ball gown, a crown, royal jewels, and loyal subjects to come to the royal ball.
    [1. Play—Fiction. 2. Imagination—Fiction.] I. Title. II. Series.
PZ7.C638Pr 1998
[E]—dc21

98-11365
CIP
AC

ISBN 0-448-41604-2   I J

PRINCESS FOR A DAY

By Maryann Cocca-Leffler

Grosset & Dunlap • New York

Last week Jessie went to
the moon in her spaceship.

4

Yesterday Jessie
climbed a mountain.

And she camped in the woods.

Today she is a princess.

She has a crown to prove it.

And tomorrow there will be
a Royal Ball.
She makes invitations.

Come to a
Royal Ball!
It will be at 9:30
in the morning.
Wear your best
gown.

She gives the invitations
to all her loyal subjects.

Later Princess Jessica
gets the royal garden
ready for the ball.

Then she finds
a ball gown.
She puts gold bows
on her shoes.

The next morning
Princess Jessica comes downstairs.
She has on all the royal jewels.

"Jessie, why are you wearing
a curtain?"
asks her sister Kelly.
"My dear sister,
<u>I</u> am Princess Jessica.
And <u>this</u> is my ball gown,"
says Princess Jessica.
Kelly rolls her eyes.

"Queen Mother,"
says Princess Jessica.
"What will we have to eat
at the Royal Ball?"
"Will milk and muffins do?"
Mom asks.
Princess Jessica nods.
"The Royal Ball must end
at 12 o'clock," says Mom.
"Uncle Steve is taking you
out to lunch."

Soon the Royal Ball begins.

All the loyal subjects
wear their best gowns.
They sip milk
from pretty teacups.

They dance and sing.

They even ride
the royal horse.

At noon Princess Jessica
waves good-bye to everyone.

Princess Jessica runs
into the house.
It was the best ball ever!

Just then Uncle Steve arrives.
"I found this on the front steps,"
he says.
"I think it belongs to
Princess Jessica," says Mom.

"So this is Princess Jessica!"
says Uncle Steve.

"Well, let's see if the shoe fits."

"It fits! It fits!"

shouts Princess Jessica.

"My prince has come!"

Uncle Steve bows.
"Now we will go
for a royal pizza," he says.
Princess Jessica takes his hand.
"Jessie, you can't go out
like that!" Kelly calls
after her.

"Of course not!" says Mom.

"You forgot your crown!"